Let Them Eat Fruitcake!

The "truth" behind the world's most outrageous dessert

Anita Inquire

This book is a work of fiction. Names, characters, places, and incidents are the product of the author's imagination or are used fictitiously. Any resemblance to actual events, locales, or persons, living or dead, is coincidental.

First paperback edition November 2016

This edition September 2023

ISBN: 978-1-962715-00-3

Cover Illustration by Sally E. Garrison
Interior Illustrations by Lizzie Inquire

Originally created as a gift for my mom, Christmas 2003

Any grammatical errors are my mother's, who edited this book. Thanks Mom!

*Not legally binding penalties.

This book is dedicated to my parents, who gave me the gift of humor. Thank you for all your love, support, and of course...fruitcake!

Everything You Always Wanted To Know About Fruitcake, But Were Afraid To Ask

I had never really given fruitcake much thought before that fateful day a couple of Christmases ago. Now that I know the fascinating history behind this entity that people either love or hate, I feel I must tell everyone. Sit back and grab some hot chocolate and a piece of fruitcake (if you can stand it). This is one story you don't want to miss.

Anita Inquire

The story you are about to read is absolutely true. It really happened! My friends don't always believe me, but they should. You all should. My mom and I were both there. This is the first time we have shared the secrets of fruitcake. Get ready. You aren't gonna believe this!

Lizzie Inquire

Visit Santa!
You Just made it!
Another one! Oh man, I just want to eat my grilled cheese Sandwich
Sorry– closed For Santa's Nap
Heaven is a pair of pumps!
SHOE Attitude

I had been promising my daughter all day that she could visit Santa at the local mall. Unfortunately, I got caught up in an amazing shoe sale and we nearly missed Santa's visiting hours. We ran as fast as we could and just made it to the back of the line as they roped off Santa's visiting area. We were the last ones.

Santa was still quite jolly as he lifted Lizzie, then 8, onto his no doubt quite numb legs. He and Lizzie exchanged pleasantries, and Lizzie gave him her usual list of wishes: Baby-Real-Snot; My First Depreciating Car; and World's Hardest Clay; just to name a few.

Then Santa said, "Since you are the last one, little Lizzie Inquire, we have time if you would like to ask me any questions."

"Can it be about anything? Anything at all?" Lizzie's eyes were very wide. Santa nodded, looking extremely amused.

"Well, I do have one question that I've wanted to know my whole life," Lizzie replied.

Santa chortled, "Let me guess...why can't you have a horse or anything in the world you ask for? Why don't I grant all wishes?"

Lizzie shook her head, "No."

So hungry-
Want Grilled
Cheese!

"How do I fly around the whole world in one night?"

"No," Lizzie replied intently.

"How do I enter people's homes that don't have fireplaces?" Santa asked confidently.

"No, but that is a good question," Lizzie mused.

Santa looked puzzled. "I give up. What question have you always wanted to know?"

"Well, it's about fruitcake, Santa."

"Fruitcake?" He looked highly entertained.

"Yes, fruitcake." Lizzie had a very serious look on her face. "I don't understand it."

"You don't?" Santa laughed.

"No. Why do people give it to each other? Where does it come from, and why would anyone make such a thing?"

"I take it you don't care for it much," Santa said with a gleam in his eye.

"No Santa. I really don't like it. My mom loves it."

Santa looked up at me and winked. "Yes, yes, Anita Inquire, you have always enjoyed a good fruitcake haven't you?"

I nodded and laughed. I couldn't wait to hear what his answer to her would be.

Elf Family Portrait

Juan Elf with baby Dick Elf
Minnie Elf with baby Harry Elf

"To tell you the truth, I have always found fruitcake to be a little perplexing myself, but delicious." Santa leaned his head back and laughed uproariously. "Sit back and get ready young Lizzie, for I am about to tell you a tale of epic proportions."

"Really?" I interjected.

Santa laughed again. "It all started back at the beginning of time when I first took on my job as Santa."

Lizzie gasped, "Wow! That sounds like a long time ago. Is fruitcake that old? It kind of tastes that old."

Santa chuckled and continued. "Back then I used to make the toys myself. It was just Mrs. Claus and I. It was a simpler time. No electricity, no batteries...toys were easy."

"It was about that same time that a newly married elf couple, Minnie and Juan Elf, started a family. I didn't even know about elves back then. Never knew they existed."

"The Elf's two oldest boys were completely opposite and didn't get along at all. Harry and Dick Elf constantly disagreed and drove their parents crazy. The whole lot was actually rather miserable. In addition to the constant bickering between the siblings, none of the elves were fulfilled."

Your mama has pointed ears!
All of our moms have pointed ears.
We have The same mom, dummy!
duh!

Santa continued, "Harry was a couple of inches shorter, and wore solid colored elf pants. His brother Dick was the taller one, and believed all elves should wear striped pants. Over time, they each started a gang."

"There were elf gangs?" Lizzie looked amazed.

"Oh yes, I'm afraid so. These things have been going on for years. History does repeat itself." Santa sighed. "So the two gangs gradually built up...the striped pants gang vs. the solid colored pants gang, until the entire elf village was divided." Santa shook his head sadly.

"During that time the world was also becoming more populated, and Mrs. Claus and I felt it was time to hire some help to keep up with toy production. We started with the reindeer, but you know some creatures are just suited to one thing. They are incredible fliers and quite talented in gossip, but when it comes to building toys...not so much."

"I can imagine!" Lizzie and Santa smiled at me.

Santa continued, "Everything the reindeer built looked the same...dolls, trucks, clothes...it all looked like a rounded, clumpish piece of wood. Not very popular with the kids. Oh, I should have

I heard Blinky is dating Fizzy!
I know! You didn't hear it from me, okay?
Are you kidding me? But she's a moose!
You gonna eat those toys?
doll
Truck

known better, what with their hooves and all...not very dexterous." Santa reflected and chuckled.

"Well, there just aren't a lot of people living in the North Pole. That climate isn't for everyone. I had to start somewhere. I then tried hiring abominable snowmen, but they have terrible tempers and hunger. They either ate all of the toys they made, or threw them at each other until they broke." Santa rolled his eyes.

"Back in Elf Towne, the gang fight had escalated and The Elf Wars had begun."

"Elf wars?" Lizzie and I exchanged looks of astonishment.

"Oh yes, it was a very dark time, indeed. Fortunately, weapons were limited. They started with snow, but found it to be rather ineffective. They had grown up having snowball fights, so this was hardly appropriate for war. Natural resources were slim to none in those parts, but they did what they could. Harry's side tried using cake, of which there was plenty, and throwing it at the other elves. Dick and his gang only laughed hysterically at their efforts."

"What kind of stupid weapon is that?" Dick asked sarcastically.

SECRET LAB
Yeah, could I get a 7-layer chocolate...
Hee Hee Ha Ha Ha
Dorks!

"You trying to sweeten us to death? Ha, Ha, Ha, Ha!" He and his elf warriors then tossed little tiny pieces of fruit at the enemy side. Harry laughed at them. "Oh no! A bite size piece of fruit is headed right for me! I'm shakin' in my pointed shoes!"

I looked at Lizzie and saw her mouth hanging wide open. I then realized mine was, too. "They were fruit flinging?" I asked Santa.

"Yes, yes they were. I suppose that was probably the first food fight ever!" Santa snickered.

"Now then, each side got together to brainstorm different ideas for weapons. It was Harry's side that first thought to combine the fruit with the cake. They did several test runs in the lab to find just the right consistency to hold it all together. They didn't want it to crumble mid flight. Harry Elf and his gang used every binding agent they could find, including glue and cement."

Lizzie blinked hard, and her eyes opened even wider.

"When they were happy with the fruit cake consistency, they drilled a hole through the middle of it, placed it on the end of a pole, and ran as fast as they could to the fruitcake launching line. Harry's gang hurled fruitcake with all their might

Incoming! Arrrggghhh
Death by Fruitcake! Who Knew?
Really Fling it at them, Lenny!
Fruitcake Launching Line

at Dick's elf soldiers."

"At first the elves laughed, thinking more cake was heading for them. But they noticed the cake was holding its shape and building up speed. It appeared to be quite substantial and ominous. Dick's gang became alarmed and started to run, just as the fruitcakes hit their targets."

Santa reflected. "Oh, it was terrible! Elves were crushed under the weight of the fruitcakes. Some suffered terrible head injuries and broken limbs. Buildings were crushed under the weight of the incoming fruitcakes. Some elves thought they would eat a little...and boy, was that a mistake!"

"Indigestion?" I asked.

"Actually no, but the fruitcake was so heavy in their bellies, they were unable to run. Some couldn't even get up."

"Woo, I know that feeling," Lizzie added. "I ate too much fruitcake at Aunt Gertrude's one time, and I could barely move for a week!"

"I told her a little goes a long way."

"That's for sure," Santa agreed. "Now one of the elves, who was a bit more enlightened, but rather shy, snuck off to avoid the terrible war. I walked

North Pole
Did I hear him right? They were hurling fruitcakes at each other?
I'm Hermit. I come from a town full of imbeciles

out my front door at the North Pole and came face to face with him, one morning. His name was Hermit Elf. He told me all about the goings on, and about the fruitcake. I was horrified!"

"He didn't want to return home, so I offered him a job and a place to stay. The North Pole was quite small at that point, but we made room for him. And, my! What a talent! He was incredibly gifted at making toys and he loved it. He absolutely loved it! I remember wishing I had more elves just like him."

"Some time went by, and both opposing elf societies constructed elaborate workshops with fruitcake-making labs, and factories for mass production."

I was amazed and so was Lizzie.

"Those elves worked extremely quickly, and they too, had quite a knack for building things. They almost all have the gift." Santa looked thoughtful.

"Both sides were busy perfecting their versions of super strong, super powerful fruitcakes."

"Dick's side made fruitcake too?" asked Lizzie.

Oh, look...
a secret snow
cave!
Shhh, hide the
fruitcake here
Moan!

"Oh yes, it was the perfect weapon. Both sides continued to attack each other with fruitcake. The towns were in shambles. Fruitcakes don't biodegrade, so they just sat there on the streets. The factories were filled with them. People seem to think there is only one fruitcake that has been passed around. If they only knew...there are millions of them!"

Lizzie gasped, "Wow, that's pretty scary!"

"Indeed! Now it just so happens that a new snow cave was discovered near one of the elves' borders, and plans were being made to store fruitcakes inside of it and on top of it. What they didn't realize was that both sides had thought of this and secretly claimed it as their own. Elves from both sides were busy sneaking around hiding fruitcakes under blankets of snow on top of the cave. Harry and Dick, the leaders of the war, ran into each other one day while inspecting the inside of the cave. Each had a few men with him."

"This is my overflow area! Get out you striped pants goon!" screamed Harry.

"No way, shorty! This is my cave!" hollered Dick Elf.

An Elf, a snowman, + a deer walk into a bar, . .

"They screamed at each other for a few minutes and then a strange rumbling started. The sound grew louder and louder, and things began to shake. All at once, the cave collapsed and the entrance was blocked off."

"Earthquake?" I asked.

"No, Anita. The combination of loud screaming voices, and the weight of the fruitcakes on the cave roof, caused a mini avalanche. They were trapped inside for weeks."

Lizzie asked, "Did they die?"

"No, there was an air pocket inside and the elves were fine."

Santa continued with the story.

Dick said, "Well, I guess we could live in here for a long time. We can always eat snow and fruitcake."

"Yeah, we'll never go hungry with that stuff. It's giving me a bellyache though!" laughed Harry.

Santa reflected, "A strange thing happened to the elves in that cave."

"What?" wondered Lizzie.

"They began to see the humor in the situation. The humor of hurling fruitcakes. And in fruitcake itself. The brothers made up. The near death experience caused them to see that fighting over height and stocking color was ridiculous. They

Well, if we can't dump them into the ocean, or launch them into space, what will we do?
I dunno. Whatever you do, don't try to flush one. Oh man, that was bad!
Hmmm, they don't flush?

had days to sit and talk through it all."

"Didn't they try to escape?"

"Their bellies were too full to even move. The fruitcake forced them to just sit and talk. Gradually, they heard the sounds of elves trying to dig them out. Even outside the cave, both opposing sides found themselves getting along, as they worked together for a common cause."

"Once their friends and leaders had been freed, a truce was called. Now they just had two problems. One was that they didn't really know what to do with themselves. They had been at war for so long. The elves liked creating things, but what could they make now? The other problem was the fruitcakes. They plowed through the ones on the streets and eventually got the rest of them all stocked away in factory cabinets and supply rooms. They held meetings to see if maybe they could launch them into space, or dump them into the ocean. They learned the hard way that you cannot flush a fruitcake down the toilet." Santa grimaced.

"Word of the newfound peace made its way to Hermit who was quite overworked building toys for me, all by himself. I decided to go meet with

ELF FACTORY
North Pole
or
Bust!

the elf leaders. I explained to them about the overpopulation crisis, and that I needed more toy makers. They were overjoyed!"

"They hitched up their factories and relocated to my area of the North Pole. The elves added on a few more factories and workbenches, and soon found the job of their dreams. All of my problems had been solved, too. I was finally able to keep up with toy production. I'm still doing fine, even today, thanks to the elves and of course my online purchases."

"Online purchases?" Lizzie and I were shocked.

"Oh sure, I love to surf the web!"

"You surf?" We said in unison.

"Of course. The internet has really helped us keep up with population demands."

Again Lizzie and I exchanged looks.

Santa paused, "There was only one problem."

"What?"

"The fruitcake. As you know, you can only eat so much of it, and it never disintegrates. Every closet and cupboard was filled with them, and we needed the space to store toys. After meeting with Harry and Dick Elf, we came up with a plan. We gradually circulated the fruitcakes into the general

Bad Toupe
Pssst, does he think that toupe looks good?

population for years, as a unique Christmas dessert."

"Are they safe to eat?" Lizzie looked worried. "They're so old."

Santa laughed, "Fruitcake lasts forever my dear. It tastes the same today as it did back then. But, we can only put so many out each year, or humans would riot. Lots of people re-gift them, but eventually the fruitcakes are eaten, and we send out a few more. We estimate that by the year 3078, we will have gotten rid of them at the North Pole, and by 3278 they should have finally been consumed. We'll have to see if we want to make any more after that."

Lizzie was deep in thought. "I thought my aunt Gertrude made her fruitcake."

"Oh, a few people do. There are recipes circulating. I can give you the recipe if you like!" chuckled Santa.

"No thank you!" Lizzie now looked positively horrified.

"We do prefer people let us give them the fruitcake, but it can be a fun project to try to make your own. Now you know the truth about fruitcake and the Elf Wars. We're lucky this had a happy ending. I shudder to think what would have

Mall Exit
Your father is never going to believe this!
Now can I have lunch? I'm so hungry, I'd eat a fruitcake!

happened, had the elves continued fighting and producing fruitcakes."

"Thank you Santa." She gave him a hug.

"I'm glad you asked, my dear. You and your mom enjoy the rest of this wonderful, magical season, and I'll be paying you a visit real soon."

Lizzie got up looking rather dazed, as I'm sure I did, and we staggered out of the mall. We both decided to write down every detail of the story as soon as we got home, so we could share this amazing tale with everyone. After all, fruitcake is one of mankind's greatest mysteries. Who knew?

My husband thought we were nuts, as did most of the people we told, but we believed.

Christmas Eve came, and our family snuggled up in bed with images of fruitcakes dancing in our heads.

Christmas morning, we woke up and tore through all our wonderful gifts. As we made our way to the back of the tree, I saw it. I gasped and grabbed Lizzie by the arm. It took both of us to lift it...an enormous fruitcake in a tin. Attached was a note that read:

Is that from Aunt Gertrude?
It weighs 700 pounds!
You can eat my share!
FRUITCAKE

Lizzie & Anita,
I couldn't resist! This ought to last you awhile. Enjoy! Wink, wink!

Love,
Santa
Dick & Harry

A recipe for fruitcake was attached to the back of the note. We laughed and wondered what had been crushed, as this fruitcake had been hurled across the land at the rival elf group. Oh my, what a history!

Our family decided to have a small piece of the fruitcake for breakfast, and do you know what? It never tasted so good! So now you know.

The End

Epilogue

Anita Inquire and her daughter Lizzie, age 10 at the time of this printing, live in Arizona. They are gaining quite a bit of recognition. Most of the world has accepted this story and been thankful to finally know the truth behind fruitcake. Anita reports that there has been a small fruitcake story backlash and that their house has been egged, or rather "fruitcaked," a few times. Nevertheless, they are enjoying their fame and feel good about spreading the word. Anita has even organized a fruitcake recovery support group for both fruitcake addictions and fruitcake anxiety. She says she wants to give back to the community.

Lizzie has become very popular at school. After being voted Student Body President, she implemented new playground toys made out of...what else? Fruitcake! She still refuses to eat it, but her mom enjoys having a piece occasionally.

Mr. Inquire has finally accepted the story, and they all plan to live happily ever after.

The word on the street is that Santa is fine with the public knowing this once classified secret.

Fruitcake Recipe*

Makes a great family project!
Fruitcake lasts for years!

Supplies:

safety goggles
rubber mallet
titanium crowbar
extra heavy strength cake pan
4 cups antacid
6 cups flour
8 cups sugar
6 cups salt
13 eggs
5 lbs spare fruit chunks
8 cups water
2 cups cement
4 cups glue
7 cups rubber extract

Warning:

Always wear safety goggles, as fruit may become a projectile weapon under the pressure of the rubber mallet.

Not for those easily frustrated.

Directions:

Put on safety goggles. Mix together flour, sugar, salt, eggs, water, and antacid. Slowly stir in spare fruit chunks. Continue stirring and add cement, glue, and rubber extract. The mixture will become extremely firm. Do not fear it. Do not let the fruitcake take control. Beat the substance vigorously with a rubber mallet for 31 minutes. Hurl clump carefully into extra strong, reinforced, cake pan. Bake at 600° for 3 hours. Remove and allow to cool for 1 hour. Use titanium crowbar to remove from pan. Do not become enraged if you cannot remove from pan. Keep trying, or stick a bow on it and give to a friend or relative you dislike. If all else fails, halt baking project and write to Santa. He will gladly deliver as many fruitcakes as you want for free. Enjoy!

Makes one 57 lb, 8" circular fruitcake.

Feeds up to 912 people.

Cut into 912 1/16 lb pieces

Health Warning:

Do not eat more than 1/8th lb, as antacid is unable to counteract severe abdominal pressure and bloating.

*This recipe is purely fictitious. Not for consumption. Do not try this at home!

Fruitcake Notes and Doodles!

COMING SOON...

RIBBON CANDY: THE NINTH WONDER OF THE WORLD

By Ivanna Snoop

Everyone has secretly wondered about ribbon candy at one time or another. Why do so many older people have it in their homes? Why isn't it edible? Why is it not sold in stores? Where is it coming from?

Ivanna Snoop triumphantly solves the mystery of this candy once and for all. Follow her hilarious escapades as she and a batty old woman, named Myrtle, delve into a world unknown to most. Learn the secrets never before shared with humans...or at least *young* humans.

Published by:
The Little Bookworm's Press

For any questions, comments, or concerns,
including press inquiries please message:
thelittlebookwormspress@protonmail.com

Follow us on Instagram:
@thelittlebookwormspress

www.ingramcontent.com/pod-product-compliance
Lightning Source LLC
Chambersburg PA
CBHW040547170726
48295CB00012B/623
* 9 7 8 1 9 6 2 7 1 5 0 0 3 *